INSPIRING TRUE STORIES BOOK FOR 8 YEAR OLD GIRLS!

I am 8 and Amazing

Inspiring True Stories of Courage, Self-Esteem, Self-Love, and self-Confidence

Paula Collins

Table of Contents

Introduction

Hello! Do you realize how amazing you are?

You are exceptional. You are completely unique. Always remember that! You are the only you there is in the entire world, and that's out of billions of people!

The world has many big and small hurdles in store for you. Sometimes you might think that you can't make it. You might get very scared or doubt yourself. However, I want to tell you a secret. Everybody feels like this from time to time! Even adults.

In this Inspiring Stories book, you will meet other amazing girls. These girls overcome their fears, show great inner strength, and reveal their bravery.

Of course, you can show all these qualities too, but you must start believing in yourself. That is exactly   what this book will help you learn to do.

You can shine your light in your corner of the

world and bring that light to other people when you let go of fear and keep learning lessons. When you believe in yourself, you can accomplish anything. You are an Amazing girl.

Grandma's Piano

Emily's Great Search

Hello! I'm Emily. I am 8 years old (but I am almost 9!) and today I discovered something super important: I have no idea what I like to do! Well, that's not entirely true. I like eating ice cream and watching cartoons, but my mom says that doesn't count as a talent. (Although I think tasting ice cream would be a great job).

Everyone in my family has found something they

are passionate about. My brother is a soccer genius (although, between you and me, I think he just runs after the ball like a crazy puppy.) My mom is an amazing artist, whose paintings I don't always understand, but she seems happy. So, I decided that today would be the day I would discover my passion.

First, I tried soccer, but it turns out that running and kicking at the same time is harder than it looks. Then, I tried to paint like my mom, but I ended up painting the floor more than the canvas. Mom was not very happy.

So, what does a girl do when she doesn't know what she likes? Well... obviously start looking of course! However, If I don't find my talent today or tomorrow, it is okay. I'll enjoy my adventures (and misadventures) until I find it. Something tells me that we are going to have many funny stories to tell.

Well, who knows, maybe I'll discover that I'm a super spy or something! For now, I'm just Emily, the girl in search of her passion.

The Mystery of the Attic

Today was one of those days that makes you say: "Wow, I didn't expect that!" It turns out that I went to my grandfather's  house, which is like entering a time machine because everything there is old but super interesting.

We were looking in the attic for something that could be my hidden talent (because, of course, talents hide in attics, everyone knows that!).

Among old boxes and books that smell of adventure, we found an object covered in dust. It was... a piano! But not just any piano, it was my great-grandmother's piano, who according to my grandfather, was an incredible pianist. I wondered if musical talent is something that is inherited, like blue eyes or the ability to sleep late.

I tried to play a note and... BOOM! It sounded more like noise than music. My grandfather laughed and said we all start like that. That made me think, what if music is my thing? Imagine, me becoming a piano superstar! (Although, for now, with not scaring the neighborhood cats I'm content).

Tomorrow I will try again. After all, discovering a hidden talent is not something that happens every day. Wish me luck! Who knows, maybe the next time I write here, it will be to tell you how I became Emily, the famous pianist (or at least, the one who tries not to make noise with it).

The First Notes

Today could have been the day I gave up the piano... but it wasn't.

After my "big debut" playing for my friends (which, to be honest, sounded more like a catfight than a concert), I thought about quitting. Everyone was laughing, and I just wanted to hide under the keys.

But then, something incredible happened. My parents, instead of letting me quit, enrolled me in piano lessons. At first, I resisted. More opportunities to make noise? No thanks. But my piano teacher, Mr. López, is different. He says that all great pianists started with wrong notes and that music is like a language that you have to learn little by little.

So, here I am, learning to say "hello" on the piano. Although my fingers get tangled and the keys sometimes seem to speak an alien language, I'm starting to understand them. Today, I managed to play "Mary Had a Little Lamb" without mistakes (well, almost without mistakes).

My parents say I'm improving and that makes me think that maybe, just maybe, I might become a pianist after all. Not the next Beethoven, but maybe someone who can play a song without the neighbors running away.

Tomorrow is another day and who knows what melodies I will learn.

A New Beginning

Today was a day I will never forget. After weeks of practice, stumbles, and off-key notes, the day of the piano recital finally arrived. I was so nervous that I almost forgot how to sit in front of the piano. When my fingers touched the first notes of "The Waltz of the Flowers", something magical happened. The music flowed, and for a moment, I forgot all of my fear.

At the end of the song, the silence was broken with applause. A standing ovation! I could not believe it. My parents were there, smiling and clapping. Even my brother, who normally mocks my attempts, seemed impressed.

That wasn't all. After the recital, my piano teacher gave me incredible news: I had won a scholarship to study at a famous music academy. I, Emily, the girl who didn't know what she liked to do, was now on her way to becoming a real pianist!

Reflecting on everything that has happened, I realized how important it is to keep trying, even when things seem impossible. I learned to keep trying and to never give up. It is important to achieve your dreams, no matter the obstacles.

So, this is not a goodbye, but a "see you later." Because this is just the beginning of many more adventures and lessons I will learn on my musical journey.

Thank you for being with me on this trip!

Growing in the Team

The Big Dream Begins

Hey there! I'm Emma, I just turned the big 8, and let me tell you, sports are my thing, but soccer? That's my super thing. I live in this cool city with my parents, where there's an incredible children's soccer league that I've been eyeing. And guess what? Today is the day I step up to try out and hopefully snag a spot on the team. The selection tryouts start today and will stretch over two days, filled with challenges and opportunities to show what I've got.

For me, soccer is much more than just kicking a ball around; it's like my own superhero cape. Dreaming of being part of a star team, wearing that jersey, and doing victory dances with my teammates is just about to step out of the dream world and become a reality. The chance to join the children's league and show off my soccer skills is right in front of me, and boy, my determination is sky-high!

I've been practicing a ton. Every day, after doing homework (and I promise I do the homework first, even though sometimes I get distracted thinking about soccer), I go out to the garden and kick the ball against the wall over and over again. Dad says I'm persistent. That means I don't easily give up.

I woke up today and the first thing I did was run to tell Dad: "It's here! Finally! We can sign up for soccer today!" Dad smiled and told me to get ready quickly.

On the way to the stadium, I felt like a mix of butterflies and quick ants in my stomach. I was nervous but also super excited. Today could be the first step in making my soccer dream come true!

Well, it's time to show what I'm made of. Wish me luck!

With love and dreams of goals,

Emma

Trials and Perseverance

The soccer team tryouts were like being on one of those shows where they give you prizes, but instead of a prize, you fight for a place on the team. There were a ton of girls, over a hundred, all wanting to be one of the few chosen.

From the moment I arrived, I felt like one of those sports superstars, even though my knees were trembling like jelly. But I remembered all the times I practiced at home, and that gave me strength. I put on the captain's band on my head (the one Dad gave me) and entered the field determined.

Each exercise was harder than the last. We did things like dribbling cones, passing the ball, and even shooting at the goal. And I'll tell you a secret: I scored a goal that even the coaches applauded.

Things got tense because every time someone made a mistake, they had to leave. But I stayed there, passing each round. And when I least expected it, there were only ten girls left. And I was one of them!

At the end of the day, I was exhausted but happy. I knew I had given my best. Now I just have to cross my fingers that tomorrow will be one of those days where they tell me, "Emma, welcome to the team!"

With my sneaker, laces still tied,

Emma

The Turn of the Game

After overcoming each test and proving I had what it takes, today life threw me one of those surprise plays that no one sees coming. Instead of running across the field scoring goals, I'll be guarding the goal. Yes, not the star forward, but the goalkeeper!

At first, I felt as if instead of a trophy, they had given me a deflated ball. I had always dreamed of being the star forward, running across the field, scoring goals, not guarding them. I didn't understand why they didn't see me as the player I always dreamed of being. But then Dad, with his way of seeing the positive in everything, helped me see things another way. "Being a goalkeeper is as crucial as being any player on the field," he said. "You have the power to protect your team's goal and make game-changing saves."

So I've decided that if I'm going to do this, I'm going to do it great. I'm going to train harder than ever, perfecting my dives and saves. I'll study the best goalkeepers, learn their techniques, and understand what makes them stand out. I'm going to guard the goal with all my might because, in a way, I will be playing my own game. And who knows, maybe being a goalkeeper will teach me something that will make me even better when I finally get to play as a forward, as I've always dreamed.

Besides, being the last line of defense and having the chance to save the game with a spectacular save doesn't sound so bad. Maybe I'll even become the hero in some matches!

So here I go, into unknown territory, with my goalie gloves and my soccer shoes well tied. I'm going to be the best goalkeeper this team has ever seen!

With a mix of nerves and excitement, Emma.

Learning in the Game

After making it onto the team, with my gloves on and the goal behind me, I began to see soccer in a new way. And you know what? I became super good at understanding tactics and plays.

After a while like this, guess what: Now I am indeed the star forward of the team! All that time observing from the goal gave me a lot of perspective. Every time I defended the goal, it was as if I was playing in my head.

This crazy journey taught me that sometimes, when the path deviates, it can lead to incredible places, like the position on the field I always dreamed of. Who would have thought!

Now, when I play, I can predict what the other players will do, as if I had a soccer superpower. And that is something I would never have learned if it hadn't been for those first days with my hands guarding the net.

This soccer adventure has shown me that no matter what, you should always follow your dreams, even if it means taking on a role you never expected. And the best part is that I've not only become a better player but also a better teammate!

Here's to more goals and more dreams!

With love and a whistle on the shelf,

Emma

Teamwork

A Big Challenge Ahead

Hi, I'm Lisa, a 8-year-old girl who absolutely loves sports, especially soccer. I live in a quiet neighborhood with my best friends Sara, Johana, and Susi, right by my side. We're not just friends; we're like a little squad of soccer enthusiasts, ready to take on any challenge that comes our way.

I want to share with you the beginning of

something big. Sara and I, along with Johana and Susi, face a huge challenge this year: to win the school's soccer championship! I'm super excited but also very nervous because, let's be honest, sometimes we have trouble agreeing.

Each of us has the "her perfect plan" on how to lead the team to victory, which sounds great until we try to combine them all. And, of course, Sara is worried because, even though we practice a lot, we still need to improve in some areas.

But, hey! We are a team, and I know we can do it if we work together. Although sometimes I wonder how we're going to survive this season without becoming a walking disaster. Well, it will at least be fun to try!

Storm in the Team

Today the sky was clear, but a storm brewed in our soccer team. It started when Johana and Susi couldn't agree on how we should play. Johana had a detailed plan, with drawings and everything, on how we were going to win every match.

On the other hand, Susi wanted us to play more spontaneously, relying more on our intuition and less on complicated plans.

I was there, in the middle of the two, trying to throw ideas so we could find a middle ground. But every time I opened my mouth, it was as if I spoke in an alien language because no one paid me any attention. I felt super invisible.

So, I thought, "Lisa, you have to do something big to solve this." And the idea of talking to the coach occurred to me. I believed he could give us adult advice to fix our differences. But, oh, it didn't go as expected. When I told the girls, they got really upset. They said I was trying to take control, and that I didn't trust them to resolve our own issues.

I felt terrible, as if I had messed up big time. But after thinking for a while, I realized my intention was good. I just wanted to help and make the team work.

So, even though today was a day full of emotions and not all good, I learned something important. Sometimes, even when you want to help, you have to make sure everyone is on board with your plan.

Tomorrow I'm going to talk to the girls, apologize, and suggest that we work together to find a solution. I'm sure that if we put in our part, we can overcome any obstacle.

Storm before the Calm

After yesterday's mess, I thought nothing could be worse. But today, wow, it was like a drama, comedy, and action movie all rolled into one.

Everyone on the team was like pressure cookers ready to explode. We talked and talked, but it was as if we were on different radio channels.

Sara was super stressed seeing how we argued non-stop. But then, as if by magic, the coach appeared with an idea that left us all open-mouthed. He said, "How about working in pairs to think of ideas?" At first, we were frozen, but then a light turned on in our heads.

So, we decided to give it a try. I was paired with Susi, and although we clashed a bit at first, we gradually began to create something super special. We invented a game that was not only fun but could also help us win. Yay!

Today I realized that sometimes, when everything seems upside down, it only takes a good idea to put everything in its place. And the coolest thing is that I learned that working together doesn't always mean agreeing, but knowing how to unite our ideas and strengths to make something big.

Lessons Won

Today was the big day, the day of our final soccer game, and wow, it felt like being on a roller coaster of emotions. After we talked about our "super cool ideas," we felt ready to take on the world. We made up a game plan that was part genius and part wild fun. Our secret?

Special moves that used everything we knew. It sounded perfect when we talked about it. When we played, it was a big adventure.

Right from the start, we ran onto the field with all our energy. Our special moves, those "super cool ideas," started working like magic.

Passes that seemed tricky flew right where they needed to go, and our goals were more surprising than the best magic trick. For a little bit, we thought we could do anything.

But, even in the best stories, things don't always end just how you want. Even though we played the best we ever have, the other team was really strong. So strong. And even our special moves couldn't get us the win this time.

When the game ended, it felt like a dream was floating away. But then, something amazing happened. As we all hugged in the middle of the field, I realized we got something way better than a trophy: we became a real "team."

This season showed us that being good at soccer is awesome, but being good at soccer together is the best. Our "super cool idea" wasn't just about tricky moves or secrets, but about how we stick together, trust each other, and face challenges hand in hand.

So, we didn't win the trophy, but we brought home something you can't put on a shelf: friendship, being there for each other, and knowing that no matter what, we'll face it together. And to me, that's worth more than the biggest trophy.

Reflecting on this crazy adventure, I can honestly say this soccer season was the best ever. Not just because of the soccer, but because we got closer as a team. No matter where we go from here, I know we'll always remember the amazing time we had together.

Until the next adventure!

Matilda's New Home

Matilda's Arrival

Hello! My name is Ava, I'm 8 years old and, unlike many kids, I don't have any siblings. I live in a cozy house with my mom and dad, and I love sharing my toys, especially my stuffed animals. But today is a super special day! You won't believe it when I tell you: I'm going to have a sister my own age named Matilda! So, the idea of having a sister is incredibly exciting.

After many visits and interviews with people who ensure that Matilda will be happy in her new home, we're finally going to welcome her.

I helped decorate her room with dolls and clothes, and it turned out super cool! I even contributed some of my favorite stuffed animals to make her feel welcomed.

Additionally, I put up a poster with photos of the whole family, including grandparents, cousins, and uncles, so she could start getting familiar with them. The thought of  sharing my world with Matilda and showing her all my favorite things fills me with joy.

I was super nervous waiting to meet her, like when you're waiting for a movie to start that you've been wanting to see for ages.

When we arrived at Matilda's place, there were a bunch of butterflies in my stomach. She was there, facing away, looking out the window, and seemed as still as a drawing. When she turned around, wow! She had a face like she didn't want to talk to anyone.

I gave her a teddy bear, the cutest in the world, but she didn't want to take it. Oh! I felt a little sad. Mom and Dad also tried to talk to her, but she was super quiet. It was clear she didn't trust anyone.

After a little while, and after talking to some very kind people who help when you're feeling sad or confused, we went back home. Matilda went straight to her new room. It seemed like she wanted to be invisible. At dinner, Mom and Dad explained to me that Matilda needs time to adjust and feel safe.

So, this is the beginning of something big. I have a new sister, and I'm going to do everything I can to make her feel part of the family!

Overcoming Barriers

These first few days with Matilda at home have been like trying to put together a puzzle without having the picture on the box. Matilda is still in her bubble, and we're outside, trying to find a way for her to let us in.

Sometimes, I see her alone in her room looking at her books, and she seems as sad as a rainy day. Matilda feels this way because she had been with another family before, and apparently, they weren't kind to her, which makes her think it might be the same with us. I wish I could say something magical to make her smile.

Mom and Dad tried everything: from board games to baking cookies together. They had a

movie night with popcorn, but Matilda just stared at the screen as if she were watching a documentary about paint drying.

her the brightest ones, but she wasn't interested. And they're super cool!

I also tried telling her jokes and doing magic

tricks I learned (although the teddy bear didn't disappear as I hoped).

Sometimes, when I try to talk to her, it's like my words hit an invisible wall and fall to the ground. But I don't give up, because that's what sisters do, especially because today I had a small victory. I managed to get Matilda to give me one of her secret smiles, the ones you hardly ever see. It was when I told her we could be a duo of secret superheroes in the house. She would be the one with the power of invisibility (because she's really good at that) and I would be the one who talks to animals (although I still need to practice).

I'm going to keep trying! Someday, I'll find a way for Matilda to feel at home.

I hope she finds the missing piece to complete the puzzle soon!

With hope and lots of ideas in my head,

Ava

A New Dawn for Matilda

Matilda's story is like those movies where everyone applauds at the end.

After many weeks and with a lot of patience, she has started to bloom like the roses in Grandma's garden. She's no longer the girl who hid in her shell. Now, she and I do everything together, from dancing in the living room, doing homework together, to baking chocolate cakes that don't always turn out right (but that's a secret).

Our parents say that Matilda and I are like two pieces of a puzzle that fit perfectly. And it's true because I feel like it was always supposed to be this way. Sometimes, we sit

on the swing in the garden, and Matilda tells me stories about the stars. It seems like each one has a name and a story, and I know that's because of all the imagination she now allows to fly.

Reflecting on everything, we've learned that love

and kindness are like superpowers that can work wonders and achieve what you can't even imagine. Even the most frightened heart can learn to love over time. And Matilda, with her smile, has taught us that there's nothing a little love can't heal.

So, this isn't just the happy ending of a story, but the beginning of many more adventures we'll have. Because every day with Matilda is an adventure in itself.

With plenty of stories to tell and a happy heart,

Ava

Basketball Game

Basketball Practice

Hi, I'm Aurora, a brave 8-year-old girl who lives with my dad, mom, and my little brother Oliver. Today is the worst day ever! I have to go to Oliver's basketball practice, because dad is working and there's no one to look after me. I don't understand why I can't stay home alone; I'm eight and a half years old, I'm not a baby.

Mom says I'll "have a lot of fun" watching Oliver, but I know it's an adult trap. Because watching someone throw a ball over and over again is not my idea of fun. My idea of fun is staying home building a fort with blankets and pretending I'm a super spy with my toy walkie-talkie.

But no matter how much I complain or make funny faces, mom insists I have to go. She says it's important to "support the family" and "do things together." I would support more from my spy fort, but she doesn't understand.

So here I go, on my way to the gym, preparing for extreme boredom. Hey, you know what would be funny? If somehow I ended up playing on the team. Ha! That would be crazy!

I wish I could forget myself at home!

The basketball game

If someone had told me I would be using words like "pass" and "dribble" without yawning, I would have said they were crazy. But here I am, learning all about basketball... and it's not as

bad as I thought.

First, it turns out you can get points just by throwing the ball from a line on the ground. It's called a "free throw"! During a free throw, no one can try to block you while you are shooting. That's something even I could do!

Then there's something called a "timeout" which is when everyone stops playing and takes water and listens to their coach give instructions. And some have even given me their chips. Basketball might be the second best thing after pizza days in the cafeteria!

Oliver was running around and sweating like an ice cream in summer. He said it was called "exercising". Pff, I prefer "drawing", but to each their own.

And the weirdest thing of all, is that I've made friends with a girl who came to see her brother, like me. Her name is Mia and she has a collection of basketball stickers. Who knew those things existed? Now I want some too!

Maybe basketball isn't just a bunch of people chasing a ball after all. Maybe, just maybe, it could be a little... fun? Ugh, don't tell Mom I said that!

The Unexpected Basketball Star!

There I was, sitting, counting the gum stuck under the bleachers (I've reached 27, by the way), when suddenly, bam! Oliver says I have to play because they were short a kid on his team. Me! Have they lost their minds or what?

At first, I thought it was a joke. Me, in a uniform? I don't even like sweating! But before I could hide, mom was pushing me onto the court and everyone was cheering for me to play. Even Mia gave me one of her basketball stickers for good luck!

So there I was, running on the court like a  headless chicken, trying to remember what each player did. "What's a zone defense?" And why was everyone shouting "pivot!"? But then something funny happened. I started to... how do you say it? Oh yes! I was having fun!

And not only that, but I made a basket! Well, it was more beginner's luck than skill, but everyone applauded! Oliver was so proud he looked like he was going to burst. He said something about "natural talent", but I know it was just a lucky shot. Although I won't tell him that.

Mom was screaming and jumping so much she almost spilled her coffee. Who would have thought that I, Aurora, could be something like an athlete? Definitely, this was much better than my spy fort.

So, I think today I learned something: sometimes, the things you don't want to do can end up being the most fun. But shh! Don't tell Mom, or she'll start getting ideas about football or, worse, ballet.

The New Player

Today I woke up feeling different. I don't know if it was yesterday's basket or the applause, but something changed. I no longer see basketball as that boring game that makes people sweat a lot. Now it's... well, it's fun!

I spent the whole night dreaming of sinking threes and winning games. Even at breakfast, instead of eating my cereal, I wanted to practice free throws with the oranges (although mom said it wasn't a good idea).

And here comes the biggest news: Mom found a girls' basketball league! And she wants me to try it! Before, I would have said no before you could even  blink. But now, I don't know... I think I want to give it a shot. Mia will be there too, and after all, if I can make one basket once, I can do it again!

So I think I've learned that trying new things isn't so bad. Sometimes, they surprise you and you end up finding something you love. And maybe, just maybe, I too can be one of those girls who make basketball look cool.

Anyway, thank you for being here to listen to all this. Now, if you'll excuse me, I have to go practice. Because Aurora the Great Basketball Player has a nice ring to it!

Lilly The Skater

The Big Skating Decision

Hi, my name is Lilly, I'm 8 years old, and let me tell you something exciting! Today at the park I saw something super mega incredible: there were girls skating as if they had wings on their feet! They spun and glided so cool that I thought, "I want to be like them." So, right away, I went straight up to them and asked if they could teach me some of their super-secret skating tricks.

But you know what they did? They laughed at me! They said I was too small and that I should go play on the swings instead. As if swings were as cool as flying on skates!

I sat on a bench, discouraged, and for a minute I felt like an ice cream in the sun, melted and sticky. But then, like in the movies, I saw a shiny poster that said: "Big Skating Competition." It was a sign from destiny! I was going to enter that competition and show everyone what an 8-and-three-quarters-year-old girl can do!

I ran home with the poster under my arm and shouted it to Dad from the door. And Dad, who is the best dad in the universe, said, "Of course, Champ! Let's buy those skates first thing tomorrow morning."

So the next day, after breakfast (Dad made toast with smiley faces out of jam), we went to the sports store. It looked like a skating zoo: big skates, small skates, some with wheels that looked like donuts, and even some with lights! But the ones that stole my heart were the ones with wheels of a thousand colors. It was like my feet were going to throw confetti while I skated!

When I showed them to Dad, he just said, "Those are as bright as you are," and I couldn't help but smile bigger than the splash I make in the pool when I jump in really hard.

So, here I go, on my way home, with my new skates, imagining what the competition would be like, and how I would manage to learn those spins and twirls.

New Skates and Big Dreams

If you thought I was going to give up after yesterday, well, you're wrong! Today is the day when my super mega skating adventure begins. I have the coolest skates in the world and a mission: to conquer that skating competition!

Dad helped me put on my skates and... well, you know those videos of puppies wearing shoes for the first time? That's how I felt, moving my feet as if they had a life of their own. But Dad said, "Lilly, beginnings are hard, but I know you'll make it." And if Dad says it, it has to be true!

So there I was, in our concrete driveway, trying not to fall and looking like a flamingo on an ice rink. But after a lot of trying, I started to skate. And wow, did I skate a lot! From the kitchen door to almost bumping into Mr. Mustache, our cat. (Sorry, Mr. Mustache.)

Tomorrow I'm going to the park to practice. And this time, I won't just be a spectator. I'm going to be the star!

Lilly, the skater with rainbow wheels!

Dad asked me why I wanted to do this, and I told him that I wanted to show those skater girls and myself that I could also be a skating superstar. And he just smiled and said that I could be whatever I wanted.

So, I'm going to be a skater. And nobody's going to stop me! Let's see how I do!

Rolling Towards Victory

At the park, I put on my rainbow skates and I was determined to be as smooth as a ninja on wheels.

But being a ninja is hard. I tried to do a cool spin and ended up hugging the ground. I think the ground and I are already intimate friends.

Just when I was about to give up, a girl who was watching (let's call her "Skating Angel") came up to me and told me that I had to be "firm and confident" and to "stay stable on my skates." Did you know that words can be like a superpower? Well, they are.

With Skating Angel cheering me on, I felt like I had a motor in my skates. I got up, took a deep breath (almost swallowing a fly) and went for it. And I did it! I spun and didn't fall! Skating Angel and I did such an epic high five that it should have been in slow motion.

Then, she put on her skates and started doing moves so amazingly that for a second I thought her skates had a life of their own. She taught me some tricks and I'll tell you a secret: I think the skates are magical because somehow they helped me not to fall.

At the end of the day, I was skating better than ever. And when dad asked me how it went, I said, "Dad, I'm going to win that competition. Not only because I want to, but because I have friends who help me be stronger."

 Today I learned something super important: skating is like broccoli, you don't always like it at first, but you know it's good for you. I've been practicing all day and I almost don't fall anymore (just 5 times today, a record!).

Tomorrow I'm going to keep practicing. And if you see some surprised skater girls at the park, they're probably the ones who didn't believe in me. I'm going to make them fall off their skates with surprise!

Lilly, the skater who never gives up!

The Champion on Wheels

After several days of practicing, finally today was the big day: the skating competition. I woke up feeling like I had butterflies in my stomach, but not the nervous kind, the kind that are ready to do twirls.

I looked at my skates and thought about everything I've learned. Not just to skate, but also about not giving up, even when I fall or when someone says I can't. Oh, and I also learned that knee pads are skaters' best friends!

Dad, Mom, and even Mr. Mustache came to see me. And when I got there, the girls who laughed at me were there, looking at me with faces that said "she's sure to fall." But I wasn't worried, because Skating Angel had taught me the superpower of confidence.

When they called my name, I glided onto the rink. I did the spins, the jumps, and even a trick I invented called "Lilly's Tornado" (it's basically spinning around and looking surprised).

When I finished, everyone was applauding and cheering. Even the mocking girls looked like they had seen a skating ghost. And then, the moment that seemed like it was from a movie: "And the winner is... Lilly!"

I won! I won! They gave me some orange skates so bright that you'll need sunglasses to look at them. And the best part was when dad lifted me on his shoulders, and everyone hugged me like I was a famous teddy bear.

So, here I am, with a trophy and some new skates, but most importantly, I have something that will shine brighter than any skate: confidence in myself. And one thing is for sure, when you believe in yourself, there's nothing you can't do.

Lilly, skating towards her dreams!

New Pet

Operation Pup

Hi, I'm Vanessa, an 8-year-old girl living in a loving home with my mom and dad. I'm a huge animal lover, and I have a big dream: to wake up every morning with a puppy licking my face. Well, maybe not the drool part, but definitely the puppy part.

Today I tried again. And when I say "again," I mean for the millionth time asking Mom and Dad for a puppy. Why is it so hard? I'm not asking for a dinosaur (although, come to think of it, that would be cool).

Santa Claus let me down. He said he couldn't bring living beings because... well, because it's really tricky to take care of animals and make sure they're happy and healthy during his long journey around the world.

And my parents always have excuses: "The house will get dirty," "It will ruin the furniture," "It's like having another child." The last one doesn't make sense because a child can't be that furry... right?

Mom says having a pet is a big responsibility. She says I have to feed it, walk it, and - here comes the gross part - pick up its "presents." But I would do all that and more. I even named my future dog: Captain Woof!

For now, I'll settle for Max, my stuffed dog. I walk him, give him fake food, and tell him my secrets. But Max doesn't wag his tail, let alone chase after the ball. I think he's a bit lazy.

But I won't give up. I have a plan that's foolproof against parents. Tomorrow I'll start "Operation Pup," and I know that, in the end, Captain Woof will be more than just a dream.

The Pet Mission Continues

Operation Pup Report! Today I continued my mission to prove that I'm ready for a real dog, not just a stuffed one. And it's not that I don't love Max, but... well, you can't teach tricks to a dog that doesn't move.

After school, I made a list of everything I would need to take care of Captain Woof. The list is long: food, leashes, toys, a brush for his shiny fur, and of course, lots of love!

But my parents still aren't convinced. Mom says a puppy could chew up her favorite slippers, and Dad says dogs need a lot of exercise. But I can run a lot! Just yesterday I won the game of "who can run faster around the house." I'm sure Captain Woof won't be able to beat me.

And speaking of Mom and Dad, I overheard them talking in the kitchen. Mom said that maybe having a dog could be a good lesson for me, something about learning responsibility. Ha! I'm already super responsible. I can keep Max, my stuffed animal, clean and he doesn't even move.

So tomorrow I'm putting my new plan into action: "Operation Convince." I'm going to make breakfast for my parents and tell them all about how I can take care of Captain Woof. Wish your friend luck!

Bruno Enters the Scene!

Big news! But first, let me tell you about my conversation with Emma, my best friend. She brought me down from my cloud of puppies and rainbows. According to her, having a dog is more than just hugs and games in the park. You have to get up early for walks, even when it's colder outside than the fridge.

Emma says her dog, Flea (yes, that's her real name), sometimes gets into mischief, like chewing up her homework... I hope that doesn't count as an excuse not to do mine!

But now, the exciting part: Mom and Dad gave me the best surprise of all!

I came home from school and found a box with

holes in it in the middle of the living room. I thought, "Mom must have gotten a package and forgot to put the box out." All of a sudden, the box started moving! Mom said "open it!" I was a little scared! There's no way this could be a puppy, after how many excuses Mom and Dad have given me to NOT have a puppy. I slowly got closer to the box, then I heard a pitiful whining noise. I thought, "Is this really what I think it is?" I slowly opened the box, and guess what jumped out at me?! A PUPPY! A Siberian husky with eyes like two shiny marbles! After seeing him, I didn't think Captain Woof was fitting. I decided to name him Bruno instead because he looks strong and brave! And furry, very VERY furry!

 Mom gave me a list of tasks to take care of Bruno. It looks like the shopping list for an elephant's birthday party: food, water, walks, baths... and yes, picking up his "presents." But when Bruno looked at me with those eyes, I knew I would do anything for him.

So I accepted the challenge. How could I say no to that ball of fur that looks like a little bear?

But, between you and me, I'm wondering what mess I've gotten myself into. Mom says I'll learn a lot from this. I hope one of those things is how to convince

Bruno that the couch isn't a giant chew toy.

Tomorrow is Bruno's first full day at home! Wish your friend and her new adventure buddy luck!

Adventures with Bruno

What a day! Bruno is like a whirlwind with legs. You won't believe it, but my room now looks like a modern art exhibition with all the papers Bruno has decorated... with his teeth.

Oh! And there´s the "breakfast incident." Bruno discovered the napkins and decided they would be his morning snack. Then we had the "newspaper attack." Dad couldn't read the news  because... well, there was no news left, just confetti.

And yes, there are also the "presents" that Bruno leaves here and there. I learned to use the shovel and dustpan faster than saying "no, Bruno, no!" But every time I look at him and he gives me that look of "me? What did I do?" I can only sigh and get ready for cleaning.

But not everything is chaotic. When Bruno follows me around the house with those curious eyes, or when he curls up next to me, I know it's all worth it. Even the crazy races to the park when it seems like he's taking me for a walk and not the other way around.

Today I learned that having a pet is like having a little brother who never learns to talk but understands you perfectly. And although sometimes he makes me run more than in gym class, Bruno has taught me something super important: responsibility is big, but the love I feel for him is even bigger.

So yes, having a dog is hard work, but it's also the best adventure. Mom was right; I'm learning a lot. Above all, that unconditional love is the best gift of all, even better than a couch without bite marks.

Tomorrow is another day! And something tells me that with Bruno, every day will be a new adventure.

The Great Climbing Challenge

A New Challenge

Hey there! I'm Lily, an adventurous 8-year-old girl ready to tackle the Great Climbing Challenge at my school today. Yes, you heard right. Climbing. That thing where you climb a giant wall and pretend you're not about to turn into a pancake if you fall.

I live with my jokester dad, supportive mom, and my younger brother, who always wants to know everything about everything. I start each day full of energy, even if today's task seems more daunting than usual.

I woke up this morning feeling like an adventurer, as if I was about to discover a new planet or something. But also a bit nervous because, between you and me, heights and I don't get along very well. It's a secret, so don't tell anyone.

 I had breakfast with Mom and Dad, and told them about the challenge. Mom said it would be cool, and Dad made one of his silly jokes, saying I should bring a parachute just in case. They both laughed, but I could only smile a little. Sometimes I think they don't understand how serious this is.

Then, while getting ready, I practiced my "I'm super brave" face in the mirror. I think I did pretty well, though I was not sure my teddy bear was very convinced.

On the way to school, Amelia, my best friend, was waiting for me. She was nervous too, but together we decided that we were going to conquer that climbing wall. Or at least try not to cry. That would already be a big victory, don't you think?

So here I was, about to face my fear of heights and prove I can do anything I set my mind to. Well, almost anything. I'm still not ready to try the Brussels sprouts Mom insists are delicious. There are limits.

Wish me luck!

The Great Adventure

We arrived at school, and there it was, taller and more daunting than I remembered. Suddenly, my shoes felt like they weighed a million pounds. Is it possible to have lead feet?

Before starting, Amelia and I did our "supreme climbers" secret handshake. We made it up on the way to school; it consists of an elbow bump, followed by a motion that looks like we're climbing. It probably looked weird from the outside, but it gave us just the boost we needed.

My heart was pounding when it was my turn. I climbed the first section and looked down;

mistake number one. Everything looked so small, and my stomach felt funny. But then, I heard Amelia and my classmates cheering me on from below. I wasn't alone in this.

With every step, I felt braver. And even though my hands were a bit shaky, I realized I could do it. In fact, I was doing it. I was climbing!

 When I reached the top, I couldn't believe it. I was so excited that I shouted: "I'm the queen of the world!" (It just came out). And the view from up there... Wow!, I had never seen the schoolyard from that perspective. It looked all so... different.

Coming down was another adventure, but there was Amelia, waiting for me with a huge smile. We had done it. Not only had I climbed, but our friendship had reached a new level.

Our teacher told us that the most important thing wasn't reaching the top but having the courage to try. That phrase made me feel even prouder of what I had done.

So, today I learned that even if something seems impossible at first, with a bit of support and a lot of bravery, you can achieve anything. Oh, and I also learned that seeing the world from above is pretty incredible.

Reflections from the Top

After the big day yesterday, today was one for reflection. You know? Even though I was no longer on the climbing wall, somehow I felt like I was still up there, looking at everything from a different perspective.

In class, while everyone kept talking about the climbing challenge, I realized that what I had done wasn't just a big deal for me but also for my friends. It taught us that sometimes, to see the world differently, you just need to change where and how you stand.

I talked to Amelia about how I felt, and she totally agreed. We decided that from now on, we're going to look for more "mountains" to conquer. Not just climbing walls, but any challenge that comes our way. Whether it's learning to play an instrument, getting better grades in math, or even learning to do a cartwheel in gymnastics.

The funny part of the day was when I tried to explain to my little brother all about climbing and how it made me feel. He just wanted to know if I had seen any birds or planes from up there. Kids!

Before going to sleep, Mom came to my room and told me how proud she was of me. That made me feel even more special. It reminded me that, though reaching the top is great, it's the journey and the people who support you along the way that really matter.

So, today I learned that big lessons come from big adventures. And I'm more than ready for the next one. Who knows? Maybe one day I'll write a book about all these adventures.

Love for Animals

A Furry Beginning!

Hello!

My name is Sally, and I'm 8 and a half years old (the half is super important). I live in a place where there's always something to do, especially if you love animals as much as I do.

This morning, while walking to school, I found a kitten. And it wasn't just any kitten! It was the tiniest, most purrfect kitten I had ever seen. It looked so lonely, with its eyes like two little green marbles. So I did what any animal superhero would do: I walked up to it and said, "Hello."

Mom always says I should be careful with stray dogs and cats because we don't know if they're friendly or if they've had a bad day (like Mr. Jenkins when his newspaper doesn't arrive). But this kitten just wanted some love; I think it was love at first sight.

At school, during recess, I told my best friend Lucas about the kitten, and he said that cats have nine lives. Nine! That's like... a lot more than I have. Lucas also said that cats can see in the dark, and I thought that would be super useful for when I have to get up at night to go to the bathroom and don't want to wake anyone up.

I also tried to explain to Miss Garcia why we need  to have a "Bring Your Pet to School Day". I don't think she liked the idea very much because she started talking about allergies and rules and blah blah blah. But imagine how much we could learn about animals if everyone brought theirs. We would learn... a bunch.

After school, I convinced Mom to go see the kitten again. It was right where I left it, and Mom said we could take it to the shelter to find it a home. The shelter is my favorite place in the whole world (after the ice cream parlor, of course). But today, Mrs. Marta from the shelter seemed worried. She said they need help because they don't have enough food or toys for all the animals. And I thought, "This is a job for Sally, the animal superhero!"

So here I am, thinking about how to save the day. Tomorrow will be another adventure, and I have to be ready!

Furry Mission

Today was one of those days that just made you say "Wow!" because adventure barked at me early in the morning. After breakfast (and cleaning up the milk Robbie, my little brother, spilled again), I headed to school, my mind buzzing with thoughts of my secret plan.

At recess, Lucas tried to teach a snail how to run. It was really funny because the snail didn't even flinch. I think it was taking its nap. And speaking of naps, I almost fell asleep in history class when the teacher started talking about ancient stuff, but then I remembered the shelter!

In the afternoon, I went to the shelter with Mom, and it was like stepping into one of those movies where the hero sees that everything is upside down. The doggies greeted me with wagging tails, and the kittens purred as if they knew something was up. Mrs. Marta looked sadder than the forgotten lettuce in the fridge. She said the shelter was in trouble, that without money, they wouldn't be able to keep being a home for my four-legged friends.

Back home, I practiced my "I have a great idea" face, and I think I did pretty well. Mom almost choked on her coffee when I told her my plan. She says I'm a dreamer, but she also says that dreamers do great things. And I want to do something great.

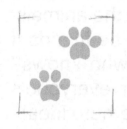 Then, I called Lucas and Maria, my best friend, and told them I needed the best secret agents for an ultra-mega important mission. Lucas asked if we had to wear disguises, and I said yes, because... why not?

Tomorrow at school, I'm going to tell my plan to the whole third grade. I don't know if they're ready for this, but as Mom says, "Nothing ventured, nothing gained!" And I'm going to win for the animals.

See you tomorrow!

Shelter Rescue Operation

If being a superhero were a contest, today I'd win the golden star. After making my bed (so Mom doesn't scold me), I went to school with my backpack full of plans and drawings of how to save the shelter.

At recess, I gathered everyone in my class around to let them know the animal shelter was struggling, but I had a superhero plan to help the animals at the shelter! Lucas wanted to know if we were going to build a fortress for the animals. Maria asked if cats and dogs could be friends. I said yes to everything because... who knows? Anything is possible. Finally, after everyone's questions, I got to tell them my superhero idea!

I said if everyone could bring dog biscuits and cat food cans to school, we could donate them to the shelter.

And then Robbie, who's always in the clouds, asked if he could bring his goldfish to keep the cats company. I don't think he understands much about cats... or fish.

After school, I went to the shelter with Mom. The animals were so happy to see us; it was like they were having a welcome party. If they could talk, they would surely tell super funny jokes!

Mrs. Marta didn't know about my plan yet, so I drew her a picture. It was me, dressed as a superhero, with a cape and everything, saving the shelter. She laughed so much that I think she forgot to be sad.

Back home, Mom helped me make a poster for school. I drew a dog shaking paws and a cat doing somersaults. Mom said that maybe that was asking too much for a cat, but I believe that with the right motivation, a cat could do anything.

So here I am, at the end of the day, with fingers full of glue and glitter, but with a heart full of hope. Tomorrow will be a great day for the animals.

See you tomorrow!

Little Paws, Big Steps

Today I woke up, and the sun was shining as if it also wanted to help the little animals. After breakfast (without milk spills, hurray!), I felt like something big was going to happen.

At school, my class looked like a pet store. Everyone brought so many dog biscuits and cat food cans that we almost couldn't fit in the

classroom! Even Robbie brought his fish... in a picture, for the cats to look at (I think he finally got the idea).

Mrs. Marta was invited as the guest of honor to our school for the "Shelter Rescue Operation" event. When she saw all the donations, tears filled her eyes... but this time with happiness. She expressed her gratitude, saying that thanks to us, the animals would have food for a while longer, and the shelter could stay open a bit more.

I learned something super important: even little hands can do big things. With just a little help from my friends, I could do something as big as... saving an entire shelter!

In the schoolyard, while Lucas tried to teach tricks to a squirrel (not very successfully), I reflected on everything that happened. If a girl like me can help so many animals, imagine what we could all do together!

See you on the next adventure.

The Skaters

Dreams on Ice

Hello! I'm Mary, an 8-year-old sports enthusiast. I live with my parents and two younger siblings. Of all the sports I love, figure skating has stolen my heart. I have a giant secret: I want to be the best figure skater in the world. Well, maybe not the best in the world because falling scares me a bit (and it hurts), but at least the best in my city. My best friend Melanie and I skate on the ice rink near the park where the ducks quack all day long. Sometimes, as we glide and twirl, I think the ducks are either cheering us on or laughing when I take a tumble – I'm not entirely sure which. But every time I step onto that ice, I feel closer to making my dream come true, one pirouette at a time.

Melanie always does spins and jumps that make me think she has wings on her skates. It's super cool! I try to keep up with her, but sometimes I end up doing the "snow angel" on the ice, which is my special way of saying I fell... again.

Oh! And there's something super important I have to tell you. Tomorrow is the tryout for our city's skating competition. I'm a little (okay, a lot) nervous because I want both of us to be chosen. It would be like a movie where we're the stars, but without cameras or popcorn.

Melanie says not to worry, that we're going to be

a dynamic duo on ice. She's brave like a superhero. I'm more like the superhero's friend who sometimes trips over their own cape.

But anyway, I'm going to sleep to dream about trophies and applause. And cross my fingers not to turn into a clumsy penguin tomorrow!

Spins and Slips

Today was THE day: the big rehearsal before the skating tryout. Melanie and I met at the rink right after school. I arrived with my backpack full of dreams and my skates... and also with a bunch of nerves!

We started warming up, which is like revving up engines before a space race, except instead of rockets, we have skates. Melanie was like a fish in water, or rather, like a skater on ice! I was more like... have you ever seen a puppy trying to catch its tail? Well, like that, spinning around and around.

I decided to try a new spin I saw on TV. In my head, it was spectacular and everyone was applauding. In reality, it was like making a sandwich, but I was the bread and the ice was the mayonnaise. Splat! Straight to the ground. But don't worry, I got up as if that was part of the plan. Melanie couldn't stop laughing, and neither could I, it was like a scene from a comedy movie!

After practicing (and falling three and a half more times), we went to register for the competition. The lady who took our information gave us a huge smile and said, "Ah, the ice artists!" That made me feel super special, although I think she remembered me because I'm always asking for ice for my bumps when I fall.

We walked home talking about how great it would be to compete together. Melanie said we would be like shooting stars, but without the danger of disappearing in the sky. I said yes, but in my mind, a shooting star surely doesn't have to worry about cosmic falls.

Well, tomorrow is the tryout and I promise I'm going to be the brightest star... or at least, the one that shines the most after laughing at her own falls.

The Big Leap

What a day! Today was the skating tryout and believe me, the ice never felt so slippery! Melanie was first. She glided across the rink as if she had engines in her skates. Everyone was watching and applauding. I was applauding too, but my hands were sweating as if they'd taken a bath.

Then it was my turn. My skates felt like they weighed tons and my legs felt like dancing spaghetti. And the whole town was there! I saw familiar faces, friends' faces, and some that I only recognize because they have funny mustaches.

I took a deep breath, and told myself, "Mary, you can do this." And then, zip! I entered the rink. I started well... for about three seconds. Then, I tried a spin and... well, I became a satellite orbiting towards the ground. Thud!

But I got up. Yes, with my pride a little bruised and my butt colder than an ice cube, but I got up. And I kept skating. Every time I fell, I thought of the park ducks, as if they were saying "quack, quack, get up!"

I finished my performance with a spin that went half okay and a bow that wasn't planned, but turned out pretty good. People applauded, and although it wasn't perfect, it was like ice cream: enjoyable even when it melts.

Melanie came running and gave me the biggest hug in the world. "You did great!" she said. I just hoped I hadn't left a puddle on the ice from all the nerves.

Now we have to wait and see if they choose us. Whatever happens, I already feel like a champion!

Learning to Skate in Life

Today was one of those days that makes you grow, although not in height (which I would like to reach for the cookie jar). Turns out only Melanie was chosen for the competition. At first,

I felt like a balloon after a party: deflated and a little sad.

I saw Melanie spinning with happiness, and I... Well, I struggled to find a smile. But then, something changed. I realized that if she was happy, I should be too. She's my best friend! So, even though I had a knot inside, on the outside I started doing the wave (even though I was alone and it wasn't very noticeable).

Later, I went to her house. When I saw her, I forgot everything else and hugged her as if she were a giant teddy bear. "Congratulations, ice star!" I said. And I meant it from the heart.

Melanie looked at me with those eyes that seemed like two shining skates and said, "Mary, without you, I wouldn't have made it this far. You taught me to get up every time I fall, even when there's no ice."

That made me feel like I had won something too... like I had won an award for best friend or something. So there we were, both of us, planning how her big day would

be. And I knew that, somehow, I would also be on that rink, skating with her in every turn and every jump.

Now I understand that sometimes, it's not about winning or losing, but about skating alongside those you love. And who knows, maybe next year, we'll both be in the competition. Because dreams, like ice cream, also come in family size!

Until the next adventure!

Made in United States
Orlando, FL
11 December 2024

55390363R00046